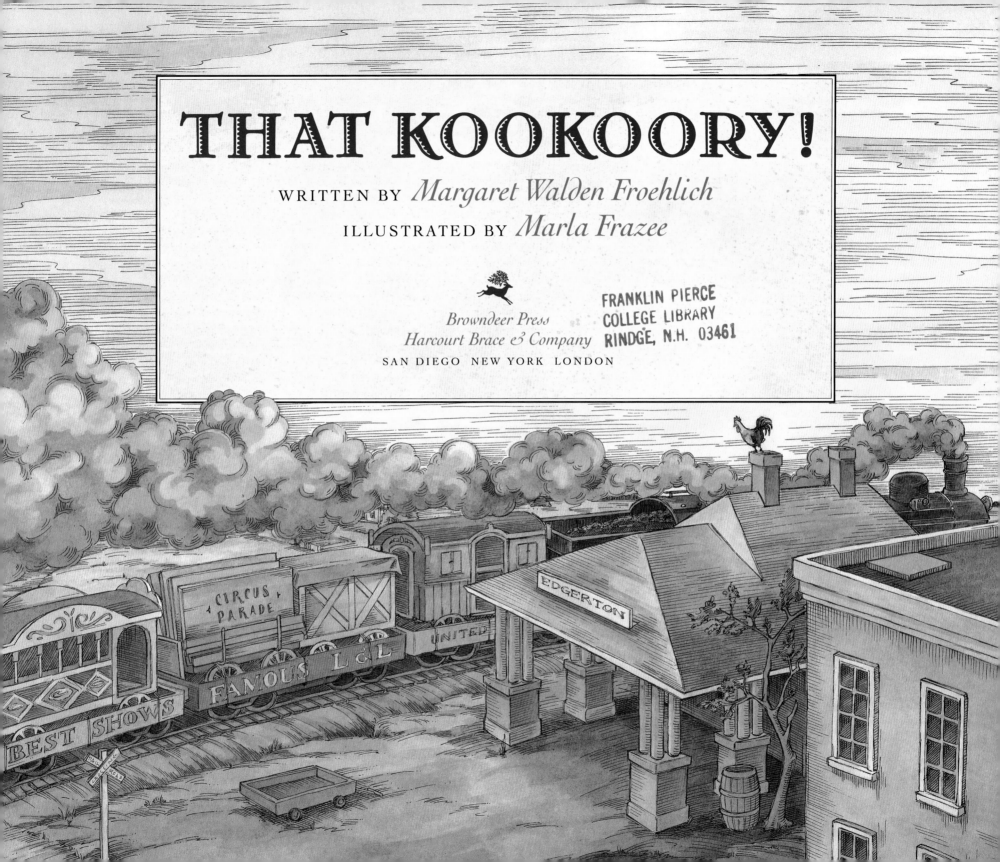

THAT KOOKOORY!

WRITTEN BY *Margaret Walden Froehlich*

ILLUSTRATED BY *Marla Frazee*

Browndeer Press
Harcourt Brace & Company

SAN DIEGO NEW YORK LONDON

Browndeer Press is a registered trademark of Harcourt Brace & Company.

Library of Congress Cataloging-in-Publication Data
Froehlich, Margaret Walden.
That Kookoory!/by Margaret Walden Froehlich;
illustrated by Marla Frazee.—1st ed.
p.   cm.
"Browndeer Press"
Summary: In his excitement about Edgerton Fair,
Kookoory the rooster wakes his friends and
inadvertently attracts the attention of a hungry weasel.
ISBN 0-15-277650-8
[1. Roosters—Fiction. 2. Fairs—Fiction.]
I. Frazee, Marla, ill. II. Title.
PZ7.F9197Th   1995
[E]—dc20   93-41833

Printed in Singapore

First Edition

A B C D E

The illustrations in this book were done in Pelikan transparent drawing inks
on Strathmore illustration board, cold press finish.
The display type was set in GrecoDeco Inline.
The text type was set in Cochin.
Color separations were made by Bright Arts, Ltd., Singapore
Printed and bound by Tien Wah Press, Singapore
This book was printed with soya-based inks on Leykam recycled paper,
which contains more than 20 percent postconsumer waste and
has a total recycled content of at least 50 percent.
Production supervision by Warren Wallerstein and David Hough
Designed by Kaelin Chappell and Marla Frazee

To my grandchildren—
Alexandra, John, and Esmé Carlson;
Elias and Blair Ednie

—M. W. F.

To my parents, Jerry and Nancy,
with love and thanks

—M. F.

Oh, those fairs!
Lemonade,
cotton candy,
guess-your-weight,
give a gander at strange sights!
HI-HO! COME TO EDGERTON FAIR!

Nobody was more excited about Edgerton Fair than the rooster Kookoory. "Elephants," Kookoory insisted, blathering about the fair, "sword swallowers, fat ladies, tawny lions, roly-coasters!"

His friends declared, "Oh, that rooster! What a pester! What a pother! What a love!"

At long last, the fair was tomorrow. Kookoory cavorted around the barnyard, crowing his head off. No wonder his goings-on attracted a weasel.

The weasel lurked under the umbrella leaves of a castor bean plant and watched Kookoory's antics. "I'll nab him while he's eating," the weasel decided, licking his lips.

Hoping to make morning come more quickly, Kookoory went to bed early without touching his supper.

Weasel bided in a rose brier outside the chicken coop. "At the crack of dawn, I'll lick that rooster's bones-o," he promised himself. Inside the coop, on his roost, Kookoory balanced first on his left foot, then on his right. He scratched his topknot and ruffled his feathers. Finally, Kookoory tucked his head into the dark under his wing. Every other minute, he looked to see if morning was on its way.

Keyed up as he was, Kookoory mistook the setting moon for the rising sun. Off his roost he jumped; out the door he flapped.

It took Weasel a peevish minute to get loose from his doze. By that time, Kookoory was steering through the mottled moonlight, blinking his golden eyes.

Like a checker piece, Weasel sneaked from shadow smudge to shadow smudge. "I'm in no special hurry, not I," Weasel said. "My chance will come."

Weasel was poised to pounce when Kookoory made a sharp left turn into a yard where a little cottage huddled, all dark.

"What? Grampy Spindleshanks not up yet?" Kookoory cried. "This will never do!"

He planted himself below Grampy's open bedroom window. "Fair Day!" Kookoory sang. "Fair Day! Tawny lions and roly-coasters! We'll dance 'Skip-to-My-Lou,' Grampy!"

Kookoory flew into the cottage and pulled a raveling on one of Grampy's bed socks to wake him. "Fair Day!" Kookoory sang again. Then before Grampy could grumble out of bed, Kookoory hopped out the window and skipped away.

"Shame to eat such an amusing fellow," Weasel murmured, tussling loose from a tangle of honeysuckle. He donned patience like a pocket handkerchief and trotted behind Kookoory.

When next Weasel gathered for a leap, Kookoory dodged in the direction of the bakery. Peering in the window, he saw the baker snoozing behind stacks of doughnuts on his counter.

The rooster burst in through the bakery window. "Wake up, wake up! It's Fair Day! Fair Day! Sword swallowers and fat ladies! I'll help you sell all those doughnuts, see if I don't!"

Before the baker could open his eyes, Kookoory crowed, "I'm off now to waken Mrs. Parsley and Babsy!"

Kookoory took flight from the windowsill. His wings carried him from lilac bush to butter bean pole, to cherry tree, to Mrs. Parsley's fence.

Footsore and dusty, Weasel eyed Kookoory's flight and smothered a groan against his own lean shoulder.

In her cottage by the fence,
Mrs. Parsley had rocked little Babsy's
cradle far, far into the night. At last,
cuddled like a dormouse under her pink shawl,
Babsy slept and Mrs. Parsley dozed.

Kookoory pecked the window. Kookoory tapped the door.
Then he lifted the latch and hollered, "Fair Day! Time for the fair!
Mrs. Parsley! Babsy! There will be balloons! Cotton candy!
Guess-your-weight!"

And before Mrs. Parsley could say, *"Sh-sh-sh,"* Kookoory flew
from Mrs. Parsley's front door to land on his feet atop a passing
wagon.

"Drat," Weasel said. To be less obvious, he slipped into the ditch alongside the road. "Follow the fellow, follow the fellow," Weasel gasped in time to his trot.

"Koo-koory-koooo, and a rah-rah-rah!" sang Kookoory to the rosy sky.

"Snick-a-snack! You, that's who!" said Weasel, one eye squinted, the other on Kookoory. "Hah-hah-hah," he panted behind his paw.

So they romped along—Kookoory riding, Weasel trotting.

Now, Edgerton Fair was a good deal yonder. Neither one nor the other had had breakfast, and they'd been abroad for a good while.

What should appear round the next bend but the prettiest cornfield. Corn tassels beckoned in the early morning breeze. Kookoory's stomach hugged his backbone. He was wiltish and puny for lack of supper the night before, and for want of breakfast. Edgerton Fair was still up hill and down dale. "I'll only stop for a bite," said Kookoory. With a reedy little cry, he plunged from the wagon and darted into the cornfield.

Weasel's tongue lolled dry and dusty. He coasted to rest, never minding thistle and burdock. "Let him stuff himself with corn—he'll be all the tastier," Weasel allowed, catching his breath. He closed his eyes to daydream of chicken dinner.

Meanwhile, Kookoory's friends had turned out for the fair. They made haste, anxious to catch up with him.

Grampy Spindleshanks, spry as a goat, wound the yarn of his bed sock as he hurried along. The yarn had gone all cat's cradle from Kookoory's tweaking it.

The baker wore his fresh doughnuts strung in a necklace round his neck. He carried two bags bulgy with powdered sugar to dredge his confections once he got to the fair.

Mrs. Parsley carried Babsy pick-a-back—little Babsy scarfed in her pink shawl against the morning breeze.

That same breeze ruffled the corn tassels where Kookoory,
with such an appetite...

where Weasel, with such an appetite...

Grampy Spindleshanks spied the dreaming weasel and frowned. The baker spied the dreaming weasel and frowned. From her perch, Babsy spied Kookoory feasting in the field, and she crowed his name long and loud.

Kookoory leaped from the cornfield.

The weasel woke and rallied. "It's now or never!" he cried.

The baker launched an eye-squinting sneezer of a cloud of
powdered sugar at the weasel.

Mrs. Parsley flung Babsy's shawl like a net.

Grampy Spindleshanks tackled the weasel and trussed him
with the purple yarn of his bed sock.

With Kookoory yodeling at the front of the procession, they bore the bound weasel to Edgerton Fair.

"We'll put him in a cage . . . ," they all agreed.

"And then we'll turn him loose," they said.

Turn him loose they did, but only *after* they'd cringed from the

tawny lion and marveled at the fat lady;

after they'd screamed over

the sword swallower's performance;

after they'd gone zippity-lu and jazz on the roly-coaster.

And, only *after* the weasel was full, for folks and tads, taken with the strange sight, had plied him with popcorn and peanuts and cotton candy.

Off Weasel skulked, grim-grumpy and burpish for a fellow who'd spent the day at the fair.

Kookoory flew up to the baker's shoulder for a ride home.

"How many days till Edgerton Fair rolls round again?" he inquired.

Before the baker had puzzled it out, Kookoory toppled, sound asleep, in the nuzzle of the baker's neck.

"That little Kookoory—such a pother! Such a pester! Such a love!" said his friends.

THE END